Please return/renew by date shown.
You can renew at:
norlink.norfolk.gov.uk
or by telephone: 0844 800 8006
Please have your library card & PIN ready

withdrawn from stock

NORFOLK ITEM

T37

G38

To Cecilia — S. B.

To Mum and Dad — M. C.

Barefoot Books
124 Walcot Street
Bath BA1 5BG

This book was typeset in Syntax Black and Jacoby ICG Black
The illustrations were prepared in gouache and paper collage

Graphic design by Barefoot Books, Bath. Colour separation by Bright Arts, Singapore
Printed and bound in Singapore by Tien Wah Press (Pte) Ltd

This book has been printed on 100% acid-free paper

ISBN 1-84148-623-X

British Cataloguing-in-Publication Data: a catalogue
record for this book is available from the British Library

3 5 7 9 8 6 4 2

Jump into January

A Journey Round the Year

written by

Stella Blackstone

illustrated by

Maria Carluccio

Barefoot Books
Celebrating Art and Story

Jump into **January**, come along with me!

teddy bear   hoods   footprints   puck   smoke   earmuffs

The local pond is glazed with ice — what can you see?

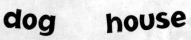

pine trees   skates   pipe   hockey stick   dog   house

Fly into **February**, come along with me!

skis   carrot   snowball   **snowman**   sledge   ski poles

The hillside glistens, white with snow — what can you see?

snow boots   *jacket*   **goggles**   *mittens*   **rabbit**   *bird*

Whirl into **March**, come along with me!

church   dog   truck   bicycle   frisbee   hats

The wind is whistling down the street — what can you see?

leaves   kite   car   clothes-line   flag   parcel

Splash into **April**,
come along with me!

boots   *puddles*   umbrellas   fountain   cat   pavement

The first spring rains are sweet and warm
— what can you see?

rain hats   steps   drainpipe   paper boat   gate   daffodils

Move into **May**, come along with me!

aprons   hoe   flower pots   trolley   rakes   cherry blossom

It's time to make our gardens grow
— what can you see?

sprinkler   hoses   trowel   watering can   fork   seed trays

Race into **June**, come along with me!

scooter   thermos   picnic rug   basket   butterfly   swing

It's so much fun to eat outdoors
— what can you see?

skateboard bread bicycle bananas cooler picnic bench

Jive into **July,** come along with me!

juggler   dolls   dodgem cars   ice cream stand   candy floss

The fair is full of games and rides — what can you see?

carousel   balloons   flags   ticket booth   ferris wheel   moon

Sail into **August**,
come along with me!

sailboats   buckets   fisherman   crab   beach ball   sunglasses

The sand is soft, the sea is warm — what can you see?

spade   seagull   hammock   surfboard   sandcastles   flippers

Slide into **September,**
come along with me!

bus teacher lunch boxes book skipping rope football

It's time to go to school again
— what can you see?

backpacks   poster   slide   hopscotch   hula hoop   squirrel

Twirl into **October**,
come along with me!

donkey   beehive   baskets   tyre swing   apples   plums

The orchard trees are full of fruit
— what can you see?

pears   pumpkins   wheelbarrow   bucket   ladder   sheep

Sweep into **November**,
come along with me!

bonfire rake birdhouse shutters lantern spectacles

**The leaves are dancing as they fall
— what can you see?**

overcoat   cat   piano   tree house   sack   broom

Dance into **December,**
come along with me!

candles   party lights   glasses   streamers   drum   presents

Let's celebrate the turning year,
and everything we see.

cakes poinsettia stockings candy canes saxophone bottles

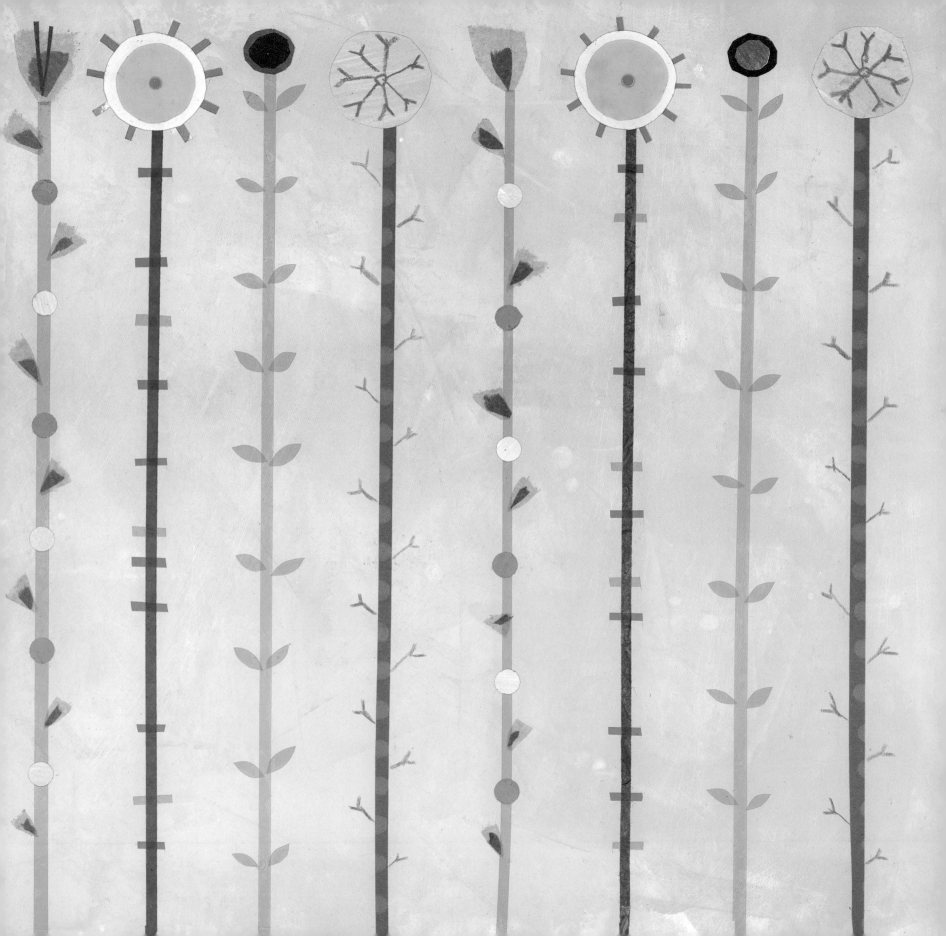